This book belongs to

....

First published in 2013 by Miles Kelly Publishing Ltd
Harding's Barn, Bardfield End Green, Thaxted, Essex, CM6 3PX, UK

2 4 6 8 10 9 7 5 3 1

Publishing Director Belinda Gallagher
Creative Director Jo Cowan
Editorial Director Rosie McGuire
Senior Designer Joe Jones
Production Manager Elizabeth Collins
Reprographics Stephan Davis, Jennifer Hunt, Thom Allaway

ISBN 978-1-78209-291-9

Printed in China

British Library Cataloguing-in-Publication Data
A catalogue record for this book is available from the British Library

ACKNOWLEDGEMENTS

The publishers would like to thank the following artists
who have contributed to this book:

Cover (main): Mélanie Florian at The Bright Agency
Decorative banners (cover and throughout): asmjp from Shutterstock.com
Insides: Richard Morgan

Made with paper from a sustainable forest

www.mileskelly.net   info@mileskelly.net

www.factsforprojects.com

Snow White

Miles Kelly

One day a queen sat sewing beside a window. As she sewed she pricked her finger, and a drop of blood fell onto the snow outside

Snow White

the ebony window ledge.

"I wish for a daughter as white as snow, as red as blood, and as black as ebony," she said to herself.

When her daughter was born she had snow-white skin, lips as red as blood and hair

Story time

as black as ebony, and she
was named Snow White.

Then the queen died and
the king married again. His
new wife was vain and very
cruel. Every morning she
would look into her magic
mirror and say, "Mirror, mirror

Snow White

Story time

on the wall, who is fairest of
us all?"

And the mirror would reply,
"Thou, oh queen, thou art
fairest of them all."

Years passed, and Snow
White grew into a lovely girl
with a gentle nature.

Snow White

One morning the queen asked her mirror the usual question, but the mirror's

reply filled her with envy.
"Oh queen, Snow White is the
fairest in the land."

The furious queen ordered
her woodsman to kill Snow
White. But he could not bear
to do so. Instead he hid Snow
White deep in the forest.

Snow White

Snow White wandered for miles, until she caught sight of a house among the trees. The door swung open at her touch. She stepped inside to find a table set with seven

plates and cups. Seven chairs were ranged round the fireplace, and along the wall

Snow White

were seven little beds. Snow White sat in a chair, and before long was fast asleep.

Now the cottage belonged to seven dwarfs and when they came home, they found Snow White. She awoke with a start, but she soon saw they were kind. She told them how she came to be in the forest.

When they heard her sad tale the dwarfs invited Snow White to stay with them, and she happily agreed. Every day the dwarfs went out to work, and they warned her never to open the door to anyone.

Then one day, back in the castle, the queen asked, "Mirror, mirror on the wall, who is fairest of us all?"

But the mirror replied, "Oh queen, Snow White with the seven dwarfs does dwell, and she is fairest of them all."

So the queen, disguising herself as an old woman, sought out the dwarfs' cottage and knocked at the door.

Snow White remembered the dwarfs' warning, and did not let the old woman in.

"I only want to
give you a delicious
apple," said the queen, and
she took a bite out of it.

So Snow White took the
apple, not realizing that the
queen had poisoned it on one
side only. The minute she bit

into it she fell down dead.

When the dwarfs came home, they found Snow White. They placed her in a glass coffin, and put it in a pretty, sheltered part of the forest.

Years passed. Snow White lay in her coffin, looking as

beautiful as ever, and the dwarfs watched over her. One day they found a young prince kneeling by her side.

He had fallen so much in love with Snow White that the dwarfs agreed he could take the glass coffin back to his palace.

As they lifted the coffin, the piece of poisoned apple fell from her lips, and Snow

White breathed again and opened her eyes.

The prince wasted no time in asking Snow White to marry him. She agreed, as long as the dwarfs could come and live at the palace as well.

The next day the wicked queen asked her mirror the usual question. To her horror it replied, "Snow White, who marries her prince today, is the fairest in the land."

The queen was so ugly in her rage that the mirror

cracked into bits. And she could never look in a mirror again as long as she lived.

The End